The BIG BAD WOLF and Me

DELPHINE PERRET

Sterling Publishing Co., Inc.
New York

Translated from the French by Shannon Rowan

Library of Congress Cataloging-in-Publication Data
Perret, Delphine.
[Moi, le loup et les chocos. English]
The Big Bad Wolf and me / Delphine Perret.
p. cm.
Summary: When the Big Bad Wolf is mistaken for a dog, he comes to live in a boy's closet and eat chocolate chip cookies.
ISBN-13: 978-1-4027-3725-1   ISBN-10: 1-4027-3725-4
[1. Wolves—Fiction. 2. Pets—Fiction.] I. Title.
PZ7.P4328Big 2006   [Fic]—dc22   2005031460

2 4 6 8 10 9 7 5 3 1

Published in 2006 by Sterling Publishing Co., Inc.
387 Park Avenue South, New York, NY 10016
© 2005 Éditions Thierry Magnier
First published in French by Éditions Thierry Magnier • Translated from the original French *Moi, le loup et les chocos* •
English translation copyright © 2006 by Sterling Publishing Co., Inc. • Distributed in Canada by Sterling Publishing
c/o Canadian Manda Group, 165 Dufferin Street, Toronto, Ontario, Canada M6K 3H6 • Distributed in the United
Kingdom by GMC Distribution Services, Castle Place, 166 High Street, Lewes, East Sussex, England BN7 1XU •
Distributed in Australia by Capricorn Link (Australia) Pty. Ltd., P.O. Box 704, Windsor, NSW 2756, Australia

Sterling ISBN 13: 978-1-4027-3725-1   ISBN 10: 1-4027-3725-4
Book Design by Richard Amari

My thanks to Tian

CLICK

CHAPTER *1*

Usually, when I get home from school, nothing exciting happens.

Oh, don't look so sad.

Come on.
Let's go get a snack.

And that is how
the Big Bad Wolf (the real one)
came to live in my closet.

Good night.

See you tomorrow.

The hardest part was keeping him a secret from all my friends. With a wolf in my closet to brag about, I could *really* have been a show-off at school.

CHAPTER 2

Mom kept asking me why I suddenly had such a giant appetite,
so I had to be more careful.

Come out of there!
    It's time to eat.

CHAPTER 3

Some days were really hard. He was one stubborn wolf.

Hey, what do you think of
the name **Zorro**?
'Cause if I had a dog,
I'd definitely name him Zorro.

But Mom won't let me get a dog.

My name's Bernard.

Hmm.

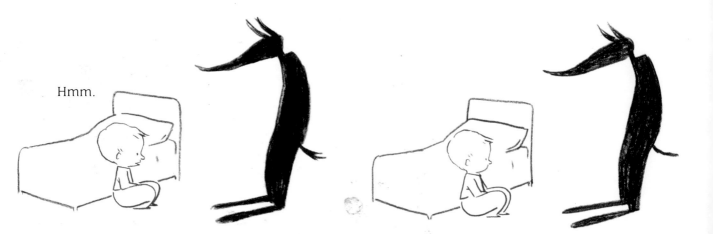

But...the problem is...
Bernard is the name of my
great-uncle—the one who
smells like soap.

So...

I was thinking...
Zorro is a much better name.

GRUMBLE

**I already told you.
My name is Bernard.**

I'm hungry.

I saved the cookies from my lunch.

One for you and one for me.
But, see, if you'd let me call you Zorro,
you could have both of them.

So…what do you think?

No? Oh, well…more for me!

CHAPTER 4

It was really fun to be the teacher for a change.

Look. The wolf there is
running after the fresh meat.
That's the wolf.
He has to be
very scary, see?

Watch this.

ROARRRRR!

Hey!

Zorro!

Where'd you go?

Come on!
You could at least try!

Okay, it's your turn now.

Yip! Yip! Aroooo!

Um...that was
a good start, Zorro.

Now let's try it with a flashlight.

CHAPTER 5

Sometimes I had to cheer him up when he was feeling discouraged.
After all, Zorro was my friend.

Hey, what's the matter?

I just tried to eat
your sister.

That's great!
Go for it!
She's a real pest.

Yeah, but I couldn't do it!

It's not such a big deal.
Why are you so upset?

I'm a failure.

I'll never scare anyone!

 Sniffle

Oh, stop.
You aren't going to cry now are you?
You're too big to cry.

But if I don't eat children, no one will respect me. I'm the Big Bad Wolf. Who'll be afraid of me if all I eat is chocolate chip cookies?

You can't give up now, after all we've been through.

We're going to keep at it. It'll be okay. You'll see.

Come on. Let's go watch TV. It's almost time for your favorite show. And Mom filled up the cookie jar again before she left.

CHAPTER 6

I always wondered what he did while I was at school.

Grrrrr

GRRRR!

Sheesh.

I need more practice.

!

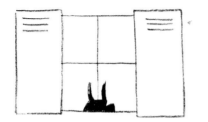

Darn!

I almost had it!

BOO!

Chapter 7

Sometimes, we both wanted to be the boss.

Zorro!

Come see.

I had a super idea.

?

I found something for you.

Okay,
you just take care of yourself then.

You **grouchy old wolf!**

NO more cookies for you!

SLAM!

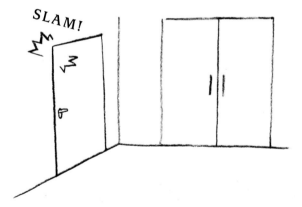

Creeeeak

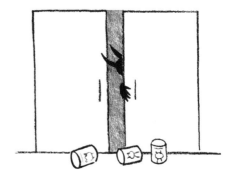

Ah...do I smell salmon?

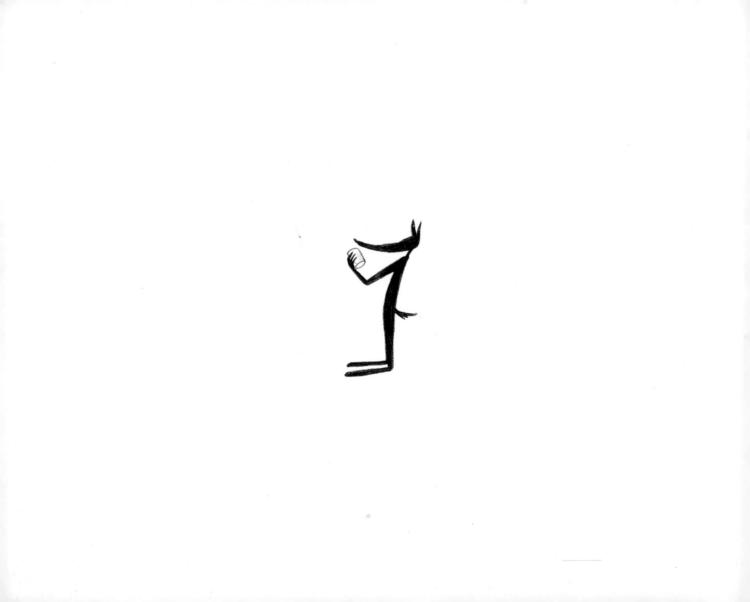

CHAPTER 8

Most of the time, we had lots of fun.

You can't get me, pale face!

Give up!

I've got you covered.

Wait a minute...

But…

Take off the boots.
Lemme see.

Well?

Bah…
no fair.

CHAPTER 9

Then little by little, Zorro started to make some progress.

Well, it's **bedtime** now.
Do you want me to check
your closet for monsters?

No, no, no!
Definitely not!
I mean...no thanks, Mom.
It's okay. I'm not afraid.

CLICK

Good night.

Good night,
Zorro.

CHAPTER 10

We were finally making *lots* of progress.

Hi! I'm home!

Zorro! I said I'm home.

Zorro? Are you there?

Creeeeeak

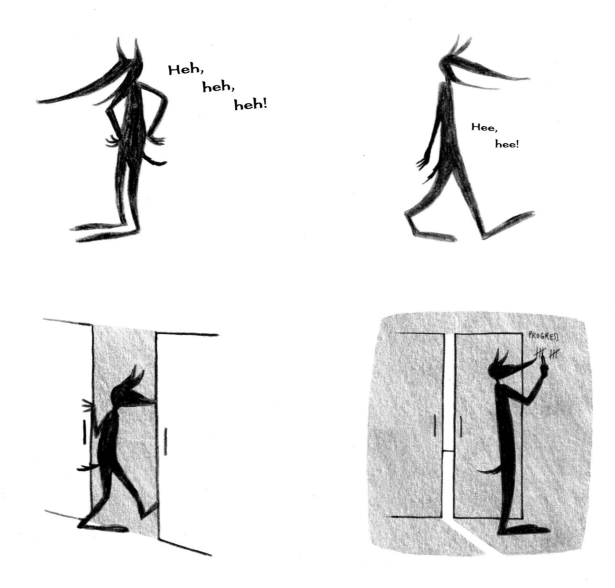

CHAPTER *11*

The next morning I set a new record for getting to school FAST!

CHAPTER 12

I had to hand it to him. His hard work had really paid off.

So? How did I do?

You were amazing!

Everyone at school
was terrified of you.

How does it feel to be
the **Big Bad Wolf** again?

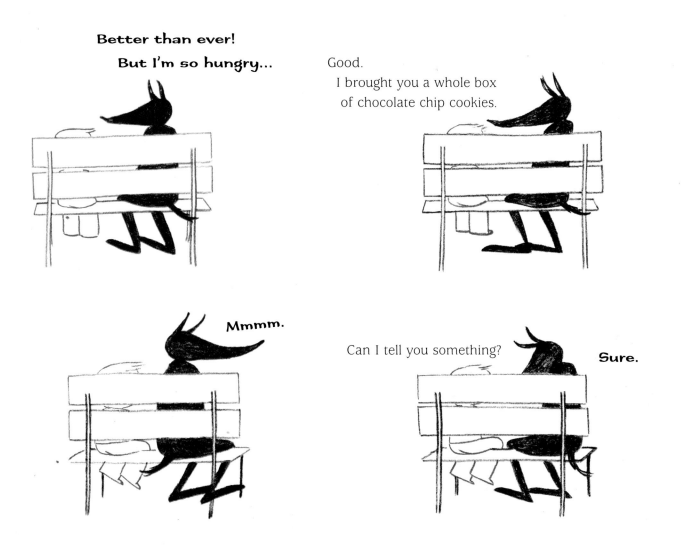

If I ever got a dog, I would definitely name him Bernard.